To the beautiful state of Ohio and to all the readers who enjoy discovering
the rich heritage of the first people who settled here.

Dandi

To my mother, Mick, 90 years young, and my children—
Tom, Elise, and Ben—whose greatest years are ahead of them.

Greg

I'd like to acknowledge the work of Dr. Barbara Mann, an author and expert
on oral tradition and a professor of Native American Literature, Department
of English, at the University of Toledo. Her work has inspired mine.

—Dandi Daley Mackall

Sleeping Bear Press

310 North Main Street, Suite 300
Chelsea, MI 48118
www.sleepingbearpress.com

© 2005 Thomson Gale, a part of the Thomson Corporation.

Thomson, Star Logo and Sleeping Bear Press are trademarks
and Gale is a registered trademark used herein under license.

Printed and bound in Canada.

10 9 8 7 6 5 4 3 2 1

Library of Congress Cataloging-in-Publication Data

Mackall, Dandi Daley.
The legend of Ohio / written by Dandi Daley Mackall ;
illustrated by Greg LaFever.
p. cm.
ISBN 1-58536-244-1
1. Iroquois Indians—Folklore. 2. Legends—Ohio.
I. LaFever, Greg, 1952- ill. II. Title.
E99.I7.M19 2005
398.2'089'97550771—dc22   2005006022

About The Legend of Ohio

This story of bravery and sacrifice is loosely based on Iroquois oral tradition. I was honored to create a version of this wonderful tradition. It relates the movement of the earliest Native Americans at the end of the last Ice Age. Oral traditions are stories passed by word of mouth, from one generation to the next. "*Keepers*" (oral traditionalists) know the stories and pass them to new generations of listeners. There are various kinds of keepers. *Firekeepers* are administrators. *Faithkeepers* keep spiritual matters. And *Keepers of Old Things* are historians, entrusted to pass along the traditions and stories.

Some of the details are taken directly from the original story, passed down through Iroquoian oral tradition, along with descriptions, such as "The Moving White Stone Mountains" and "The Grandfather Mountains." Other story details I've invented, including the young girl, Dikewamis; the use of the *atlatl* (Ohio's ancient people used the tool for sending spears long distances in the hunt); and the timeline, which compresses this complex history for the sake of story.

Rivers continue to play a vital role in Ohio today. The state has over 25,000 miles of named rivers and streams and a 451-mile border on the Ohio River (Algonquian for "beautiful river"), which is believed to have been formed by the glaciers. My hope for *The Legend of Ohio* is that all who read the story will appreciate the contributions of Ohio's brave ancestors, and appreciate the gifts of Ohio and its rivers.

—*Dandi Daley Mackall*

Before people paddled down the "Beautiful River," before the rivers reached into the green valleys beyond the Allegheny Mountains, and plantations, farms, and cities grew up along the river banks, there was a rich land waiting to be discovered—the land we now call Ohio.

In the North, the people had lived for centuries in harmony with the earth, hunting caribou and bison in the tall grasses. Young Dikewamis and her friends had splashed in streams and raced deer through forests.

But the winds began to blow strong from a frozen sky. Ice formed like mounds of white stone and slid over the face of the earth.

And the time of the Moving White Stone Mountains came to the land of the North.

The once-green earth turned to cold stone. Dikewamis and her mother planted seeds, but the seeds would not return plants. The waters hardened. And worst of all, earth's creatures fled the land.

Dikewamis and her father watched as, day after day, sharp-nosed shrews and short-faced skunks scurried southward beside lean dire wolves. Even the giant tortoise and sloth plodded south, staying ahead of the Moving White Stone Mountain.

"How will we survive, Father?" Dikewamis asked, as the thunder of musk ox, bison, mammoths, and mastodons grew fainter and more distant.

Her father gazed at the gray sky. A silvery sleet fell on his broad face. "We will trust our great Chief Tarachiawagon. He will hold up the sky so the White Stone Mountain will not swallow our people."

Dikewamis wondered how the Chief could hold up the sky, when its pieces seemed to be falling to the ground, making the White Stone Mountain grow bigger and bigger.

The next day, Tarachiawagon assembled the people. "We must follow the creatures of earth on a great journey. I have had a vision of a rich and fertile land, carved by a beautiful river. I have seen fingers of waters, softening green hills and valleys in a new and wonderful land. There, our people will find new life."

Dikewamis said goodbye to her home, turned white by the Moving Mountains. For many sunless days and moonless nights, she walked beside her mother over the frozen earth.

At last, when Dikewamis feared she could go no farther, she glimpsed on the horizon, dark mountains rising from the earth and disappearing in swirls of sky. These mountains were not like the Moving White Stone that still crept behind her people. These were true mountains, formed of rock, not ice.

"They are the Grandfather Mountains," her father told her. "We will be safe in their shelter."

They followed Tarachiawagon over the jagged rocks to the safety beneath the cliffs.

Tarachiawagon bid his people settle and rest, nestled in the foothills on the other side. Here the earth, though small in size, compared with the land of the North, was soft and green. With the skills of the beaver, Dikewamis' father built their home of sticks and bark. Dikewamis and her mother collected seeds and berries. They dug pits to store nuts. Warriors took up stone-tipped spears and *atlatl* to hunt bison, musk ox, and caribou. At night, Dikewamis listened as storytellers spun tales of bravery and honor.

Could this be the land of Tarachiawagon's vision? Dikewamis wondered. The earth fed her people. But there were no fingers of water, no beautiful river.

As one planting season after another passed, more and more travelers found their way to the land beneath the Grandfather Mountains. The people outnumbered the bison, and herds grew thin. Dikewamis' father no longer returned from the hunt with a share of the white-tailed deer or caribou.

Still they came, making their homes on crowded land that grew more barren with every passing moon. Colors faded from the earth. Once again, all life began to ache with hunger. Dikewamis' mother scraped turnips for supper and shared beaten roots with the elders.

Dikewamis wondered how the great Chief's vision could have been so wrong. Where were the fingers of water to feed the earth? Where was this rich and fertile land he had promised his people?

Then one day, Dikewamis woke to a *chink, chink, chink*.

Tarachiawagon stood at the edge of the White Stone Mountain that had followed them from the North. A crowd gathered. Yet no one questioned the great Chief. With one hand, he held a jagged stone knife, shaped like a willow leaf, firm against the ice. With his other hand, he brought down the hammerstone, his movements steady as footsteps.

Chink, chink, chink.

Day after day, by sun and by moon, Tarachiawagon struck the ice, sending tiny shards flying like crystal embers.

"Why does our Chief chip at this white stone?" asked Dikewamis' friend.

"Why can he not find food for us instead?" complained another.

Moons passed, and Dikewamis did not see a single white-tailed deer or hear the thunder of bison. Even the turnips and nuts grew scarce.

And still, Tarachiawagon *chink, chink, chinked* on his piece of the White Stone Mountain.

"Father," said Dikewamis, hunger swelling in her belly, cold and solid as ice, "what will become of our people?"

Father looked to the sky.
"Tarachiawagon has kept us in safety
from the Moving White Stone. We will
trust in him again. He is our Chief."

Every day Dikewamis and her father joined the crowd gathered around Tarachiawagon. He scraped the ice with the hard point of a caribou bone. The jagged ice gave in to the power of the Chief's mighty hands. Slowly, a form took shape in the ice—long and narrow, rough and hollow in the center.

Dikewamis watched as Tarachiawagon set large branches into flame, then lifted the burning tongues of fire to lick the ice-stone carving. Water dripped to the earth, gathered in pools, then raced together down the hill and out of sight.

Dikewamis and her people
followed the river. Soon instead
of only one river, many fingers
of water spread out farther than
the eye could see. As if a hand had
clawed the earth, the rivers of water
snaked through hills and valleys, marking
the paths of the great Chief, who had
discovered a new home for his people.

The waters led them to rich lands, where soft earth welcomed their seeds, and plentiful grass fed the bison and white-tailed deer. They settled into every corner of this promised land. Dikewamis and her people called the new land, "Ohio," which means "Beautiful River."

Glossary

Allegheny Mountains [AL-i-GA-ne]: A 500-mile mountain range, stretching from northern Pennsylvania to southwest Virginia, with the western portion extending into Ohio and Kentucky. The range makes up the western part of the Appalachian Mountains.

Atlatl [at-LAT-l]: An ancient weapon used before the introduction of the bow and arrow. It added force to the spear by launching a flexible dart, rather than simply using the hand-thrown spear.

"Beautiful River": The meaning of "Ohio" in the Algonquian language. Native Americans used this Iroquois word, "Oh-ee-yo," to describe the river that forms Ohio's southern border.

Bison [BI-sen]: Buffalo

Caribou [KAR-e-boo]: Large reindeer, native to North America

Dikewamis [Di KAY wah mish]: An ancient, Native American name

Dire wolves [dir]: Large, wolf-like mammals that lived in North America during the Pleistocene Epoch, thousands of years ago.

Elders [EL-drz]: Older members of a family or tribe, given respect and a place of honor in the community.

Faith: A confident trust, or belief; the conviction of things hoped for and unseen.

Fertile [FUR-tl]: Rich, productive, able to produce crops.

Giant tortoise [TOR-tis]: Type of large, terrestrial turtle, existing since ancient times.

Grandfather Mountains: The Alleghenies. Native American oral tradition referred to the Alleghenies as the Grandfather Mountains.

Hammerstone: An ancient implement, or primitive tool, like a stone hammer.

Horizon [he RI zen]: The line where it appears to the observer that earth meets sky.

Mammoth [MAM eth]: Large, hairy elephant, now extinct.

Mastodon [MAS te-don]: Large, extinct mammal that looked somewhat like an elephant with long molar teeth.

Moving White Stone Mountains: Glaciers. Native American storytellers sometimes refer to the glaciers that moved across the continent during the Paleolithic Era, or Stone Age, as "Moving White Stone Mountains."

Musk ox [MUSK oks]: Large, stocky animal, similar to the ox, but shaggy, and giving off a musky smell.

Shards: Pieces of broken glass or pottery, or ice.

Sharp-nosed shrews: Small mammals, with pointed noses; the oldest type of shrew.

Short-faced skunks: Ancient variety of skunk; a meat-eating mammal.

Sloth [sloth]: Slow-moving mammal with hooked claws.

Tarachiawagon [TAR-e-chi-WA gen}: The name for the Creator in certain Native American traditions, namely Mohawk; also, the name bestowed upon a revered Chief. Translated, the name means "The Man Who Holds the Sky" or "Holder of the Heavens," or "He Who Holds the Heavens."

White-tailed deer: State mammal of Ohio. The white-tailed deer inhabit every county in Ohio.

Vision [VIZH en]: A mental image of something extraordinary.

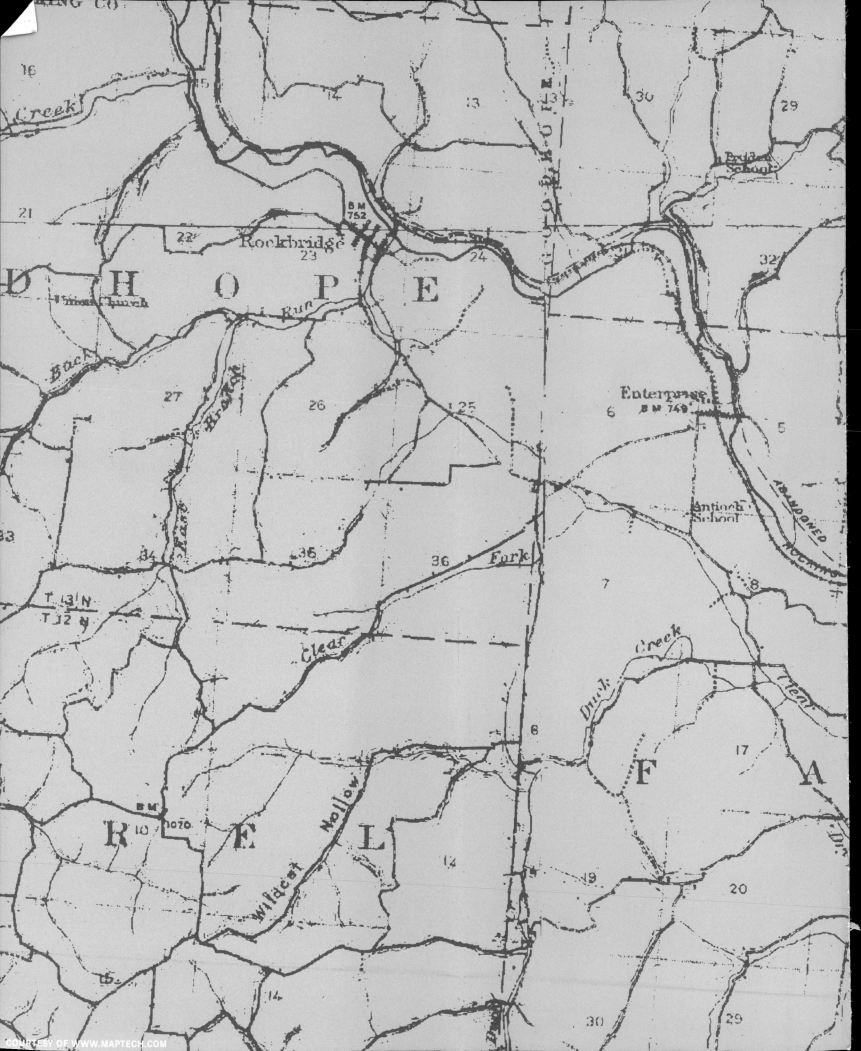